Favourites from
Andy Pandy's
Annuals

Autumn

Winter

THE BUBBLE BURSTERS

ANDY Pandy rummaged about at the back of the toy cupboard. "Look what I've found, Teddy!" he said. "A bubble pipe!"

Teddy came to look. "If we had another one," he said, "and some soapy water, we could blow bubbles. May we, Andy?"

But Andy was already looking into the toy cupboard again. "I knew we had two," he said, holding up a second clay pipe. "So we can blow bubbles. There's just time before bed."

He fetched a small pudding bowl, and poured some soap-flakes into it.

"I'll put some water in, and you stir, Teddy," he said.

Teddy could hardly wait to begin. He loved doing things with water. He dipped his pipe into the pudding basin, and blew as hard as he could. A stream of coloured bubbles floated out of the pipe and into the air.

"Look, Andy!" shouted Teddy, jumping up and down. "Look at my lovely bubbles!"

He stopped shouting long enough to blow another stream into the air. Andy laughed, and blew some himself, and soon the room was full of bubbles floating in the air until they burst.

"Why do they burst, Andy?" asked Teddy. "Why can't we keep them for ever and ever?"

"I don't know, Teddy," said Andy. "They just do, and a good thing too,"

Then they put their bubble-pipes back in the toy cupboard, and went upstairs to bed.

"Look!" said Andy, while he was brushing his teeth. "Toothpaste makes tiny bubbles too. No, Teddy, DON'T make them on purpose."

But it was too late. Naughty Teddy had made a frothy moustache, and was making faces at himself in the glass.

"Andy," said Teddy, a little while later, snuggling down in his bed, "we still don't know why bubbles burst, do we?"

"No," said Andy sleepily, "and I don't expect we ever shall. Goodnight, Teddy."

"Goodnight, Andy," said Teddy,

he went on, laughing, "because we shouldn't really like to live in a house full of bubbles all the time, should we?"

"No . . . o . . . o," said Teddy slowly, "but some of the time would be nice."

"Some of the time is just what we're having," said Andy. "Now then, just one more blow, then we must go up to bed."

So Teddy blew into his pipe once more. The biggest bubble they had ever seen floated gently into the air, and fell on to Teddy's head, where it burst with a small pop, leaving a small damp patch on his fur.

"We know what made THAT bubble burst, anyway," shouted Andy. "It was you!"

with a big yawn, and a moment later they were fast asleep.

Teddy woke with a start a little while later when something damp touched his face. He sat up and rubbed his eyes. Then he rubbed them again, as well he might. The room was full of enormous bubbles. One floated past his face, and he put out a paw to touch it. Much to his surprise, the bubble didn't burst, but just floated gently away again.

"Bother!" said a voice. "I missed that one!" and Teddy saw a tiny man standing on his eiderdown. He was about three inches high, and he had a funny little pointed hat and pointed shoes. In his hand was a long needle.

"Andy!" called Teddy. "Wake up! The room is full of bubbles, and there's a little man with a needle standing on my bed."

"Nonsense, Teddy," said Andy in a sleepy voice. "Little men with needles don't stand on people's beds in the middle of the night. Go to sleep."

"It ISN'T nonsense," said Teddy, looking all round him, "and there isn't one little man with a needle. There are lots and lots of them, and they're flying about."

And so they were. There were so many that Teddy couldn't even begin to count them, because he counts on his paws, and he only has four.

"Wake up, Andy!" shouted Teddy again. "There are so many little men that I haven't enough paws to count them."

6

"You're quite right, Teddy," said the little man on his eiderdown. "It would be very hard to count us even if you had hundreds of paws, because we move about all the time. We have to, you see," he went on, "because bubbles just won't stay still."

He broke off to go springing after one that had floated past him. He pricked it with his needle, and there was a tiny pop as it exploded.

"You see," said the little man. "We're jumping about all the time."

By this time Andy Pandy was awake too, and staring in a surprised way at all the bubbles and at the little men busily bursting them.

"Would you like to try?" asked the chief bubble-burster, handing his needle to Andy. "I can always use my hat and my shoes," he went on, and there were two more tiny pops as he pricked one bubble with his pointed hat and another with one of his shoes.

"So THAT's why they're so pointed," said Andy and Teddy together.

"Of course it is," replied the little man. "When you think of all the bubbles that little boys and little bears make every day you'll see that just our needles aren't enough."

"Do you mean to say," asked Andy, "that you have to burst all the bubbles that Teddy makes when he cleans his teeth, and sometimes even when he drinks his milk through a straw?"

he added, looking hard at Teddy.

"Oh, yes, indeed," said the little man, "and the ones you make when you do the washing, or when you play with your bubble-pipe. Think what would happen if we didn't. You wouldn't be able to move about for bubbles. The house would be full of them. That's why we're always so busy."

While he was talking, he was jumping up and down, bursting bubbles left and right.

"Why don't we ever see you?" asked Teddy, watching Andy chasing a big coloured bubble with the needle.

"You can only see us at night," said the little man, "and, of course, you're usually asleep at night." He laughed as Andy missed the bubble he was chasing. "It's not as easy as it looks, is it, Andy Pandy?" he said. "But you're coming on very nicely, especially as you can't fly. Would you like to be a bubble-burster like me?"

"I'd rather be a little boy, and make bubbles for you to burst," said Andy.

The little man laughed. "Quite right too," he said. "After all, if little boys didn't make bubbles, we shouldn't have any work to do, should we?" Still

laughing, he glanced round the room. There wasn't a single bubble to be seen. "All right, men," he called, clapping his hands. "We'd better get on with our next job," and as he said this all the little men shouldered their needles and flew out of the bedroom window, followed by the chief bubble-burster, who waved his hand as he went.

Andy and Teddy climbed back into bed.

"Just think," said Teddy. "Every time I blow bubbles in my milk with a straw."

"And every time you make frothy moustaches with your toothpaste," added Andy, laughing.

"And when we do the washing," Teddy went on.

"And when we blow bubbles with our clay pipes," they shouted both together. "Oh, those poor little men! We'll never blow bubbles again!"

But they did, of course, because when they woke up next morning they had forgotten all about the little men with their funny pointed hats and their little pointed shoes.

But next time you blow bubbles, you'll remember them, won't you?

TEDDY
AND THE
TIN-OPENER

A big parcel came for Andy Pandy and Teddy. "What can it be?" said Andy. "It isn't Christmas and it isn't a birthday." It was a tin of biscuits.

"What a lovely surprise!" cried Teddy, who is very fond of biscuits. "May we open it now this minute?" He didn't wait for an answer but raced into the kitchen.

He put the tin on the table, and got out a tin opener. But try as he might he couldn't open that tin. "Andy!" he called. "All these lovely biscuits are wasted."

"I can't get them out of the tin." He sounded very sad. "Teddy," said Andy, trying not to laugh, "it's not that sort of tin. Give it to me, and I'll show you."

He just lifted off the lid. Teddy was rather cross. "But a tin-opener OUGHT to open tins," he said. Andy knew how to make him smile again. "You may have two biscuits," he said.

"Why don't all tins open with lids?" Teddy asked. Andy Pandy didn't know. Do you? You just think. What about tins of soup or fruit?

CORK TOYS

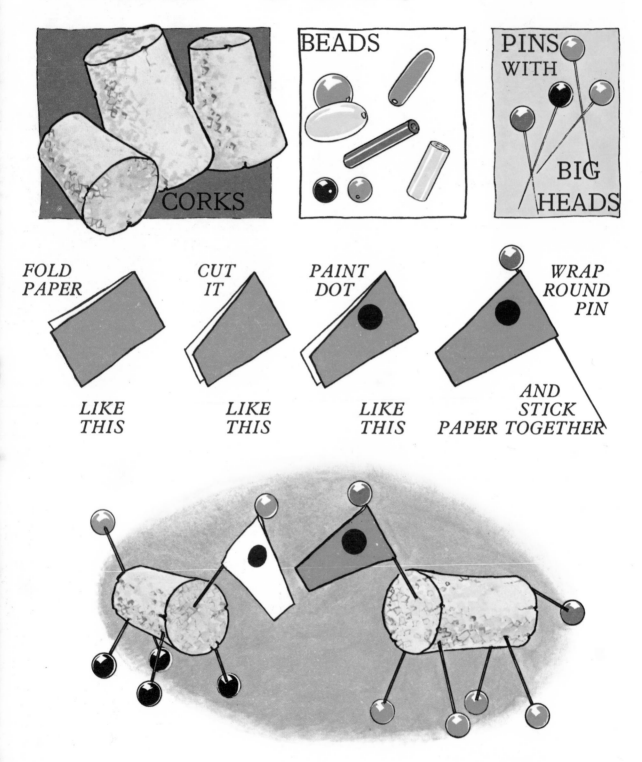

CORKS

BEADS

PINS WITH BIG HEADS

FOLD PAPER *LIKE THIS*

CUT IT *LIKE THIS*

PAINT DOT *LIKE THIS*

WRAP ROUND PIN *AND STICK PAPER TOGETHER*

PINS, CORKS AND PAPER MAKE HORSES THAT WILL STAND

SQUARE OF PAPER

DRAW THIS ON PAPER

CUT IT OUT

HERE IS A FLOWERPOT WITH FLOWERS

BEADS, PINS, A CORK AND A PAPER FACE MAKE A LITTLE DOLLY

CORKS STUCK TOGETHER, PINS AND PAPER SAILS
MAKE A BOAT THAT WILL FLOAT

A PICTURE TO PAINT

Can you find six things missing in the lower one?

THE RESCUE

Andy and Teddy were creeping on all-fours and being careful not to make a sound.

Teddy held his breath until his fur stood on end, trying, to be quiet, but then he had to let it all out again with a great big gusty sigh. Andy turned round with his finger on his lip to warn him to be more careful. Neither of them noticed that the White Kitten had left the wigwam and was following behind, chasing Teddy's peacock's feather as it trailed along in the grass behind him. Suddenly he pounced on it. Teddy started up in alarm. He didn't really believe there were other Indians in the garden, but someone or something seemed to be pulling his head backwards.

"Andy!" he shouted at the top of his voice. "Look at my head! It's being pulled off."

Andy Pandy turned round. Then he burst out laughing. There was the White Kitten sitting on the end of the peacock's feather, and there was Teddy with his head pulled back and not able to see what was happening.

Andy Pandy went to pick up the kitten and Teddy said that he hadn't really been frightened, because he knew that there were only pretend Indians in the garden. "I think I'll walk the rest of the way," he went on. "Then the White Kitten won't be able to reach my feather."

They started off again, the White Kitten prancing along with them and every now and then jumping up to try to reach the feather bobbing along behind Teddy. Andy Pandy was in front. When they came in sight of the wigwam it was his turn to wonder whether his pretend Indians had turned into real ones.

"Look!" he said, staring hard.

Teddy did look. So did the White Kitten, whose tail once more stood upright, with every hair bristling. The whole wigwam was rocking and bulging as if it were full of Indians, all fighting each other.

"Whatever is it?" Andy Pandy whispered, as he and Teddy clutched each other and stared at the wigwam billowing about like a ship at sea.

Teddy began to cry. "I wish we had never played Indians," he said. "I didn't think they would turn into real ones."

"Let's go a bit closer," Andy said, taking a step forward.

"No, no!" cried Teddy. "They might come after us."

By this time Andy Pandy, who was a very sensible little boy, had got over his first surprise. He said bravely to Teddy: "Of course it can't be real Indians. Perhaps it's a dog who has got into the wigwam and can't find his way out."

He went slowly towards the wigwam, and Teddy followed, keeping very close. The White Kitten too crept along, taking tiny little steps but still waving his tail angrily in the air.

Suddenly Andy Pandy noticed that the flap of the wigwam was closed. he had left it open. Even as it, something that looked like a feather at the bottom of the wigwa.. fly in again. Then he heard a noise, and he stopped short.

"It's geese, Teddy," he said. "It's

the geese belonging to the farm who have got into the wigwam. Look, the flap has fallen down and they can't find their way out!"

"I don't like geese," Teddy said. "They make hiss noises, and they peck."

"I don't like them much," Andy answered, "but we can't leave them in there."

"How shall we get them out?" Teddy asked.

Andy said: "If I can get the flap open, they'll find their way out."

But he didn't go at once, beca he hoped the great noisy geese would come out by themselves. They sounded so angry that he thought they would rush at the first thing they saw when they did get out, and if that thing happened to be Teddy or himself . . . !

Suddenly he thought of something. "Looby Loo!" he shouted. "She's in there with the geese. They'll tread on her."

He rushed forward, but poor Teddy was so frightened that he could not move.

"Don't go in, don't go in!" he cried, stretching out his paws towards Andy Pandy.

But Andy did not need to go in. He remembered that he had left Looby Loo propped up against the side of the wigwam. He ran round to where he thought she was. Getting down on his knees, he pushed his hand under the canvas and felt about for her.

As soon as the geese saw a hand coming through the crack between the bottom of the tent and the grass, they rushed about and made more noise than ever. One of them actually pecked at Andy Pandy's hand. Drawing it quickly away, Andy lifted the edge of the wigwam and caught sight of Looby's shoe.

As quick as lightning he put his hand in again and snatched her out. Then he sat on the grass for a few moments with her in his arms, looking anxiously to see whether she was hurt. Her hair ribbons were undone and one of her shoes was half off and her little spotted skirt was covered with bits of grass which the angry geese had torn up and tossed about, but she seemed to be all right. When Andy had put on her shoes and tied her ribbons and picked the pieces of grass off and given her a good hug, she looked as smiling and pretty as she always did.

All this time, the geese were inside, hissing and stamping and pushing the sides of the wigwam out into all kinds of strange shapes.

Andy Pandy ran round and put Looby Loo into Teddy's arms. "Take her into the garden," he said, "and don't come near the wigwam."

Teddy started off at a run, but he could not bear the thought of leaving his dear Andy Pandy alone with the angry geese, so, when he had gone a little way, he stopped and looked back.

Andy was creeping round the tent on his tummy. He had seen that the cord, which he used if he wanted to close the flap when he was inside, was lying on the ground outside. Very quietly he wriggled towards it. Then he reached it. Crawling back, he hid round the side and gave the cord a sharp tug and pulled the flap back.

Instantly the geese rushed out, hissing and squawking more than ever. Teddy's knees shook, but he stood still while the geese flew in all directions. He had to make sure that Andy had not been pecked or trodden on. When he saw him stand up and begin to tie the flap of the tent back, he ran towards him with his arms outstretched.

"Andy," he cried, "you really and truly are a brave!"

"You are a brave too," Andy said, "for you came back to see that Looby and I were safe, and I know you must have been frightened."

"Yes, I was," Teddy said.

"We won't put the wigwam up in the field again," said Andy. "Let's take it down and have it in our own garden."

"And let's begin now," said Teddy, beginning to pull out the pegs of the wigwam.

"Very sensible!" said a voice. They didn't hear it. All they heard was the bleat of a black-and-white goat as it slipped through the hole in the hedge and went back to the farm.

As for the geese, they were so anxious to get away that they forgot they were tired and waddled back as fast as they could, not even noticing that they were being followed by flocks of little birds who flew above them twittering, "Silly geese, silly geese!"

FIR-CONE PEOPLE

If you go into the country in the autumn look on the ground for fir-cones. Some will be short and fat, and some will be long and thin

To make fir-cone people to play with you will need some stiff paper, some raffia or string and some glue and a pair of scissors

CUT A PIECE OF PAPER ABOUT THIS SIZE AND CUT LITTLE SLITS ALONG THE BOTTOM EDGE

FLATTEN OUT THE SLIT PIECES

PAINT A FACE ON IT

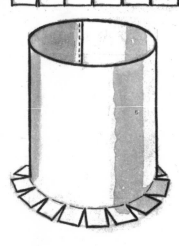

ROLL IT INTO THIS SHAPE AND GLUE IT AT THE BACK

GLUE INSIDE THE HEAD

STICK ON SOME RAFFIA FOR HAIR OR SHORT PIECES OF STRING

TURN THE HEAD UPSIDE DOWN
AND PUT A DAB OF GLUE ON EACH
LITTLE FLAT PIECE

TURN THE HEAD THE RIGHT
WAY UP AND STICK THE
LITTLE FLAT PIECES ON TO
THE FIR-CONE

THEN CUT OUT A PIECE
OF STIFF PAPER FOR A
SKIRT AND WRAP IT
ROUND THE FIR-CONE

IF YOU CAN FIND
A BIG WOODEN
BEAD, PAINT A FACE ON IT
AND GLUE IT ON TO A FIR-CONE

PLAYING
CRICKET

"Look what I've found, Teddy," said Andy Pandy one day. "A cricket bat. We had some stumps somewhere too." Teddy wanted to play straight away.

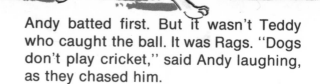

Andy batted first. But it wasn't Teddy who caught the ball. It was Rags. "Dogs don't play cricket," said Andy laughing, as they chased him.

Just look at Teddy! He tied two cushions to his legs. "Real cricketers wear pads," he said. "I'm ready now, Andy." But of course he couldn't run with those fat cushions on his legs.

He went head over heels on the grass. "We're not very good at cricket, are we?" said Andy. And as he spoke, Rags ran away with the ball again.

By the time Andy had caught Rags and untied Teddy's cushions they had to sit down. "We'll just play ball," said Andy. "That will be easier!"

"But first we have to catch Rags," said Teddy. And by the time they had caught him they were too tired to play with the ball.

1. CUT OUT SHAPES
LIKE THESE FROM OLD SCRAPS.
2. DRAW A FACE ON PAPER.
3. PASTE ON WOOL FOR HAIR.
4. PASTE HAT ON TOP OF HAIR.
5. PASTE ON JERSEY AND BOW.
6. DRAW 2 ARMS, PASTE ON GLOVES.
7. PASTE ON SKIRT.
8. DRAW 2 LEGS.
9. PASTE ON
SHOES.

Rag'Bag POLLY

MAKING FACES

Poor things! They have only got one eye each. Can you give them the other one?

HOW MANY BIRDS DO YOU KNOW?

SPARROW

CHAFFINCH

BLUETITS

ROBIN

STARLING

THRUSH

WREN

BLACKBIRD

TEDDY'S ROMPERS

1. "Andy!" said Teddy one day. "You have rompers and Looby Loo has a dress, but I haven't any clothes at all."

2. "But you have your own lovely fur," said Andy Pandy, "and a fine big red bow as well."

3. But Teddy wanted rompers, like Andy's.

4. Andy Pandy found an old blanket and got out his sewing things.

5. Teddy stood very still while Andy measured him.

6. Then Teddy helped Andy Pandy to sew the rompers, and very soon they were finished.

7. Teddy was very proud of his rompers. He stood in front of the looking glass for a long time, gazing at himself.

8. Then Andy Pandy said: "We've been indoors too long. Let's go out into the garden, Teddy."

9. They went out and began to play with their football.

10. Teddy got very, very hot, but he wouldn't take his rompers off.

11. The football sailed high into the air, and landed on the shed roof. "I'll get it," said Teddy.

12. He scrambled up the ladder and threw the ball down to Andy. Then there was a loud tearing noise. "Andy!" shouted Teddy. "I'm caught on a nail. And my lovely rompers are torn."

13. Andy Pandy sewed a big blue patch on the seat of Teddy's rompers.

14. Teddy stopped crying. "They look even nicer than before," he said.

FIND TEN HIDDEN THINGS

Can you find the ten toys and creatures hidden in this picture?

They are Andy Pandy, Rabbit, Dog, Ball, Shoe, Teddy, Cricket Bat, Engine, Tortoise, Book

The Red Squirrel

EVERY NIGHT, when Andy and Teddy go to bed, they see that Looby Loo is warm and cosy in her cot and that the White Kitten is safely in his basket, then they jump into their beds and pull the sheets and blankets up to their chins and look round the room.

'I can see the man in the moon,' Teddy said. 'He's looking in.'

'I can see thousands of stars,' Andy replied. 'They're all looking in, too. Let's count them.'

He began counting, but as Teddy can only count up to four he very soon left off and listened to Andy Pandy's nice little voice saying, '. . . nine, ten, eleven.' But Andy didn't get very far either, for in no time at all both he and his friend Teddy were fast asleep.

Now although they had seen the moon and the stars looking in at their bedroom window, which was wide open, they didn't know that two bright little eyes were looking in too. They belonged to a red squirrel with a splendid bushy tail who used to climb a tree close to the window every night and watch Andy and Teddy go to bed. In the summer he used to go away when they were asleep, but now that it was beginning to get cold at night-time he found himself staying longer and longer. He used to curl himself up into a round red ball and get into a kind of little basket made by the branches, as close to the window as he could.

One night he dreamed that they had all had a wonderful pillow fight and that Andy had found an old pillow with a hole in and shaken the feathers all over him. Brushing them away, he woke up.

'Why shouldn't I go in?' he said to himself. He leapt lightly from the branch on to the window-sill. Everything was still and quiet, but he saw that Looby Loo had her eyes wide open although she didn't move. All he could see of Teddy was a bit of yellow fluff, and Andy Pandy looked like a little hill because he was rather fond of sleeping on his front with his behind stuck up under the bedclothes.

The red squirrel jumped on to the end of Andy's bed, and as his bushy tail swept across the pillow Andy stirred and turned over. The squirrel took a flying leap to the floor and settled under the

bed. At that moment the White Kitten woke up and heard the faint patter of the squirrel's feet, and as his ears were very sharp he went under the bed too to see what it was; so there were the two little animals staring at each other in the blue dark.

'Hullo,' said the White Kitten.

'Hullo,' said the red squirrel.

'What do you want?' asked the kitten.

'It's cold outside,' the squirrel answered. 'I came in to play. I thought we might have a pillow fight.'

The kitten's eyes shone. 'I don't know why you should have thought that,' he said, 'but it's a splendid idea.'

'How do we get the pillows?' the squirrel asked. 'Shall we wake Andy and Teddy?'

'Ooh, no,' the kitten whispered, 'much better play by ourselves. Let's go and see which is the easiest one to get.' He crept out, with the squirrel after him, and they climbed up on to Teddy's bed.

'He's hardly using his pillow at all,' said the White Kitten, and he took one corner in his sharp little teeth and gave it a little tug. Then the squirrel took another corner in his sharp little teeth and he gave a little tug, and in a few minutes the pillow was free. Teddy didn't even stir.

The next thing was to get the pillow on to the floor. 'We can't play here on the bed,' the kitten said; 'they might wake up.'

While he was talking he jumped down on to the floor and stood on his hind legs and tried to reach the pillow, but he just wasn't tall enough. So the squirrel stood on *his* hind legs and *he* just wasn't tall enough. 'There's nothing for it,' said the kitten, 'we shall have to stand one on top of the other.'

'I'll go to the bottom,' the squirrel said, 'then you can climb up my tail and stand on my shoulders or my head, but mind my ears, because I take a lot of trouble with the tufts of hair on them and don't want them spoiled.'

So the White Kitten took great care not to disarrange the squirrel's ear-tufts. He stood up on the squirrel's head and, taking a corner of the pillow

in his sharp little teeth, he gave a tug.

'Come under the bed,' whispered the squirrel. 'It's safer there.' Between them they managed to drag the pillow with them.

'In the dream I had,' the squirrel said, 'we played with feathers.'

'I don't know anything about your dream,' said the kitten, 'but I know how to get the feathers.'

'So do I,' said the squirrel and without saying another word, the two bad little things began to bite holes in the pillow.

Very soon they each had a good pile of feathers which they threw at each other, trying hard not to laugh out

loud. But the feathers tickled and suddenly the kitten gave a tremendous sneeze. Both the animals stuffed their paws into their mouths to stifle their laughter; they rolled about, sending the feathers far and wide. You can imagine their surprise when Looby Loo got up, marched under the bed and gave them each a good spank. The kitten shot into his basket; and after staring at Looby Loo for a moment, the squirrel got in beside him, and the two of them rolled themselves into a soft furry red and white ball.

Looby Loo picked up every single feather and pushed them back through the holes the naughty animals had bitten.

Then she fetched her little workbox and mended the holes so beautifully that you couldn't even see where they had been. It was almost light by the time she had finished.

When Andy Pandy got up in the morning, he found the pillow and picked it up. 'Teddy must have thrown it out in the night,' he said as he put it back.

From the basket the kitten watched him. The squirrel had already gone but not before Looby Loo had told him that she didn't mind his coming and sharing the White Kitten's basket on cold winter nights, but if ever she caught him biting holes in the pillows again she would pull his ear-tufts.

THE CLAY HEDGEHOG

Andy Pandy and Teddy played with some clay.

Teddy rolled his into a long strip.

Andy made a big mound of clay.

Then he found some little twigs.

And cut them into little tiny strips.

Do you see what he made?

A hedgehog

Andy and Teddy took the clay hedgehog out into the garden.

They were weeding when Teddy pointed.

"Look, Andy," he shouted. "The hedge-hog is walking about!"

Andy WAS surprised.

Then he looked hard. "It is a real one, Teddy," he said.

FILL IN THE SQUARES
TO FINISH THE PICTURE

SPOTS AND DOTS
COLOUR IN THE WHITE SPACES IN THE DRAWINGS ON THIS PAGE

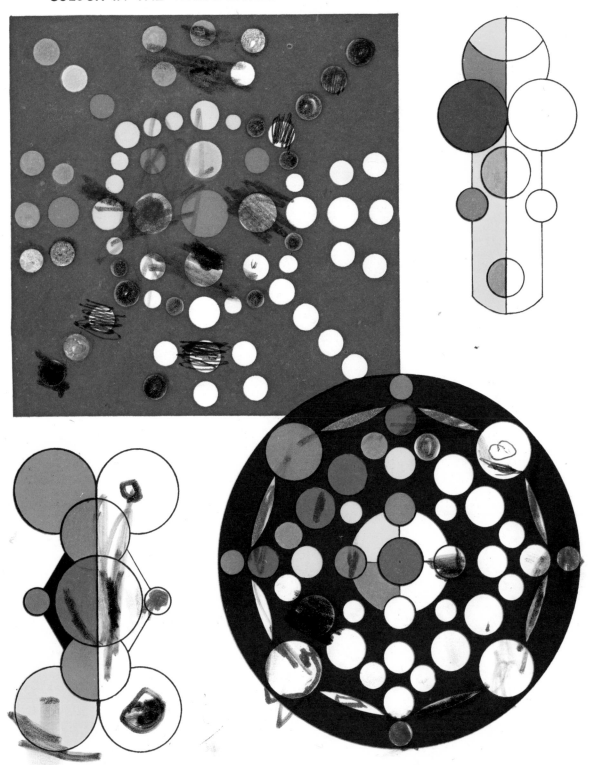

BOATS ON THE POND

1. Andy Pandy and Teddy took their boats to sail on the pond. Looby Loo went with them.

2. 'Hold the string tight, Teddy,' said Andy Pandy. 'If you don't your boat will blow away.'

3. The toy boats danced away over the water, looking just like real ones.

4. After a while Andy Pandy said: 'Do you think Looby Loo would like to have a ride in my boat, Teddy?' Looby Loo looked very pleased.

5. She sailed away over the pond, with Andy Pandy holding the string.

6. Soon Teddy said: 'May we have tea now?'

7. Andy left Looby Loo sitting in the boat but he tied the string to a big stone, so she wouldn't float away.

8. But Looby Loo wanted another ride. So when Andy wasn't looking she untied the string!

9. Suddenly Teddy noticed that the boat had gone. 'Look at Looby!' he shouted, pointing out into the middle of the pond.

10. Andy took off his shoes and rolled up his rompers and waded into the pond, which wasn't very deep.

11. 'I can't *think* how Looby got out there,' he said, as he pulled the boat in. But you know, don't you?

LOOBY LOO AND THE RABBIT HOLE

YOU remember Looby Loo, don't you? She is Andy Pandy's little rag doll. When Andy and Teddy are there she is just an ordinary rag doll, but sometimes, when they aren't looking, she goes away by herself and does all sorts of nice things. But she is always very careful to be back when they look for her, sitting just where she was before, so they don't know anything about her adventures.

One day Andy and Teddy were in the kitchen, making toffee. This always takes a long time, because Teddy gets so sticky that he quite often has to have a bath afterwards, so Looby knew she had heaps of time to go out by herself.

So, taking a clean handkerchief, she slipped quietly out of the door and ran down the garden path.

"It's a very hot day," thought Looby Loo, as she went along the lane, "so I'll go for a walk in the woods, and pick some flowers if I find any. And p'raps I'll take off my shoes and socks and paddle in the stream as well."

So she turned out of the lane and into the footpath that led to the woods. It was lovely and cool, and there were speckly patterns of sun and shade on the path.

"Hallo, Looby!" said a low, cooing voice. There was a rustle of wings as one of Andy's white doves flew over her head.

Looby waved her hand and walked on. She had nearly reached the stream, and was thinking how nice it was going to be to feel the cool water running between her toes, when she heard a small voice from the ground beside her.

"Oh, dear! Oh, dear!" said the small voice, and there was a sniffing noise, just as if someone were crying.

Looby Loo looked about her, but she couldn't see anybody. She was beginning to think that she must have been mistaken about the whole thing, when the voice spoke again.

"I want my mummy!" it said, and this time Looby was quite sure it was crying.

She looked very carefully all round her, and saw a big tuft of grass that seemed to be moving, though there wasn't any wind. So she knelt down and parted the grass, and there, in a sad little heap, was the smallest baby rabbit she had ever seen.

"You're not my mummy," said the baby rabbit, looking hard at Looby Loo.

"No, I'm not," said Looby, "but I expect I could help you find her."

"I hurt my paw on a stone," said the baby rabbit, and two big tears rolled down its soft little nose. It held its paw up for Looby to see, but though she looked at it and felt it very gently she couldn't see anything wrong with it.

"If I made a lovely bandage for your paw, would that make it better?" asked Looby Loo, and taking her clean, nicely folded handkerchief out of her pocket she tied it round the tiny paw.

The baby rabbit was so pleased to have a bandage that it quite forgot about being hurt and jumped up and down at Looby's feet, looking rather like a small, furry, bouncing ball.

"Now let's go and look for your mummy," said Looby. "Come along! I don't expect she's far away, really."

She started down the path again, with the baby rabbit lolloping along beside her.

Looby was quite right, for as they rounded a bend they came upon a big rabbit running down the path. It shot

past them in a great hurry, stopping only when the baby rabbit behind Looby shouted "Mummy!" and burst into tears again, holding out its paw as it did so.

The big rabbit stopped short and turned back.

"I hurt my paw on a stone," cried the baby rabbit.

"But I see you have a lovely bandage on to make it better," said the mother, "so it doesn't hurt any more, does it?" She looked up at Looby Loo. "Are you the kind little doll who made that nice bandage?" she asked. "I was just off to look for him," she went on. "He's always running into stones because of

not looking where he's going, but I don't think he's ever had such a smart bandage before."

"Yes," said Looby. "It's my hanky, really, but he didn't seem to be hurt very much and I didn't have a proper bandage, so I thought it would do."

The mother rabbit smiled. "He never is hurt very much," she said, "but he feels he ought to be, so he has to have a bandage to make him better. Thank you very much," she added, "and now I must go and find some carrots for lunch."

Nodding kindly to Looby Loo, and followed by the baby rabbit, she hopped off down the path.

Looby waved her hand and set off once more. After a few minutes' walk, she thought she heard the sound of running water over to her right.

"I'll take a short cut to the stream under the trees," thought Looby Loo, setting off through the thick, tangled grass and bracken.

She was just thinking how nice it was going to be to paddle her feet when the ground gave way under her. She seemed to be falling a long way, but at last she landed with a bump. It was rather dark, but she could just make out a hole in the bracken over her head.

"The hole was covered with bracken," she thought, "and that was why I fell down it. How silly of me! I don't seem to have hurt myself, anyway. That's one good thing."

As soon as her eyes were used to the dim light, she could see that she was sitting on nice, clean, soft sand, and that it would be a lovely place to play in if only there were a way out, because although it is easy to fall down a hole it is not so easy to fall up it.

Looby Loo stretched her arms above her head, but they didn't nearly reach the top of the hole. Then she tried scrambling up the sides, but the sand gave way beneath her and she tumbled down again.

"I can't jump as high as that," she said, "but I'd better try, anyway, just in case I'm a higher jumper than I thought."

But it was no good. Try as she might, Looby couldn't reach the top of the hole and scramble out. She began to feel rather worried, because Andy and Teddy wouldn't go on making toffee for ever, and when they stopped they would begin looking for her.

"It's no good crying," said Looby firmly to herself. "Crying never helped anyone, and I haven't even a hanky to dry my eyes, because I gave it to the baby rabbit."

This made her laugh and she was still laughing when a voice said "Pssst!"

Looby nodded and crawled into the tunnel. She crawled up a gentle slope for what seemed a very long time. It was almost dark, but she could just see the rabbit's white tail bobbing along in front of her. She was just wondering whether the rabbit had lost her way

A hole appeared in the smooth sand just beside Looby, and a furry face peeped through.

"I was looking for you," said the mother, "to give you back your hand-kerchief. I quite forgot just now. And it seems to me," she went on, "that I've found you just at the right moment."

"Oh, YES!" said Looby, and explained what had happened.

The rabbit looked up at the hole in the bracken. "You can't get out up-wards, but you CAN go through one of the tunnels I use to get to my home. Follow me! On hands and knees," she said, popping her head out again.

when she saw light ahead. The mother rabbit pushed aside a curtain of grass, looked cautiously about her, and then jumped out into the sunshine.

"There!" she said. "Now I must go and see if the children have eaten their carrots. Oh, and here is your handker-chief. I washed it in the stream, but I didn't have time to dry it." She handed the handkerchief to Looby, smiled kindly, and was off before Looby could even say thank you.

"Thank you, Mrs. Rabbit," Looby called, and just saw a flick of white tail vanishing down the path. "And now I must hurry," she said to herself, and ran as fast as she could back through the woods, up the lane and in at the garden gate, with her wet handkerchief in her pocket.

She was quite out of breath when she arrived home, but she knew she was in time, because she could hear Andy and Teddy laughing in the bathroom.

She had just sat down where they had left her when they came in, Teddy wrapped in a big bath-towel because his fur was all wet.

"Will the toffee soon be ready to eat, Andy?" asked Teddy.

"Quite soon," said Andy, "and then we'll have just one piece each and put the rest in the tin."

He picked up Looby Loo and saw the damp patch that the wet handkerchief had made on her dress.

"That's funny!" he said. "Looby's hanky is soaking wet, and it has sand on it."

"P'raps we left her in the sandpit yesterday," said Teddy.

"I don't think we did," said Andy. "Do you remember, Teddy?"

Teddy shook his head.

"I s'pose we must have done," said Andy, "but I don't remember at all."

"Now I'd like a piece of toffee, please," said Teddy.

Looby smiled as they went off to cut up the toffee. YOU know where that sand came from, don't you, even if Andy Pandy and Teddy didn't?

LOOKING AT THE MOON

FULL

THREE-QUARTER

HALF

QUARTER

NO MOON

QUARTER

HALF

THREE-QUARTER

FULL

Andy and Teddy say "Look at the moon." This is what it does every four weeks.

MAGIC BOXES

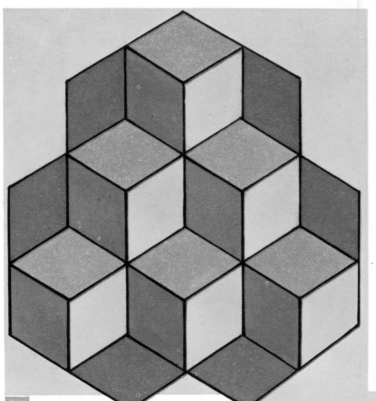

COLOUR THE
PATTERN
BELOW
AND COUNT
THE BOXES

HOW MANY
ARE THERE
—SIX?

TURN
THE PAGE
UPSIDE-DOWN
AND COUNT
AGAIN

NOW HOW
MANY
ARE THERE?

ANDY and the BROKEN EGG

1. Andy Pandy and Teddy went to the farm next to their house. They took a basket to collect eggs.

2. They went into the hen house. "Look at this great big brown egg," said Teddy.

3. "May I have it for my very own," he asked, "to keep and play with?"

4. Teddy carefully carried his egg home.

5. "Would you like it for tea?" asked Andy.

6. "No, thank you," said Teddy. "I'd like another one, please. I want to save this one."

7. When Teddy went to bed, he left his egg on the table. The white kitten jumped up.

8. He touched the egg playfully with his paw, and it rolled to the floor and broke.

9. Andy heard the noise and came downstairs. "Poor Teddy!" he said. "He will be sad."

10. Andy thought hard, then went to the cupboard.

11. He found a little yellow plush chick from an Easter egg.

12. Then he went up to bed again.

13. Next morning Teddy ran downstairs to see his egg. But he didn't mind a bit that it was broken.

14. "Look, Andy!" he cried. "There was a dear little chick inside my lovely brown egg."

TEDDY came into the kitchen one day carrying some roller skates.

"Look what I've found in the toy cupboard, Andy," he said. "May we go outside and skate straight away?"

Andy Pandy was making pastry. "Not quite straight away," he said, "because I have some little tarts to finish. But later on, if you like. What shall I put in the tarts, Teddy?" asked Andy. "You know," he went on, wondering what to say because he didn't want to hurt Teddy's feelings, "last time you tried you weren't very good at roller skating. You fell over all the time, and said you weren't ever going to skate again."

"Marmalade," said Teddy. "No, mincemeat; dear little mincemeat pies! Yes, I know I did, Andy, but that was a long time ago. I'm bigger now, and I'm sure I can do it."

Andy smiled. "All right, Teddy," he said. "I'll put the mincemeat in the pies, then you put the lids on, and we'll go out while they're in the oven."

A few minutes later they were sitting on the step putting on their roller skates. At least, Andy was. Teddy managed to fit his feet in, but he couldn't do up the straps.

"It's because my paws don't have fingers, Andy," he said, as Andy bent to help him, "but once they're on I'll manage all by myself. You'll see! Wait a minute," he cried suddenly. "I've forgotten my scarf and I'm going to skate so fast that I'll be cold without it."

"Oh, Teddy!" said Andy. "I'm not going to take your skates off just as I've put them on. You sit there. I'll get it for

you," and walking very slowly and carefully because of his skates he made his way indoors and took down Teddy's scarf.

"I shouldn't go as fast as all that, if I were you," said Andy, tying the scarf round Teddy's neck. "You'll only fall over if you do."

But Teddy wasn't really listening. "Thank you, Andy," he said. "Now I'm all ready."

He quite forgot he had skates on, and tried to jump up in his usual way. His feet flew out in front of him, and he sat down again on the step, very hard.

Andy held out a hand to help him up, but Teddy said, "No, thank you. I want to do it all by myself!"

Poor Teddy! Time and time again he tried to get up, and time and time again his feet rolled away from him and he sat down again with a bump.

Andy held out his hand again, and this time Teddy took it and was able to stand up.

"Now!" he said, and before Andy could stop him he was off down the path, wobbling from side to side and going faster and faster every minute.

"Stop, Teddy!" shouted Andy, going after him more slowly. "You're going much too fast."

Teddy's voice came back to him. "I CAN'T stop," he shouted, "and I don't think I can turn corners, either."

There was a loud splash.

"All right, Teddy. I'm coming!"

shouted Andy, skating as fast as he could towards the paddling pond.

When he got there he found Teddy on his hands and knees at the edge. His front paws were soaking wet and so was his scarf, but his feet, still wearing his precious skates, were quite dry.

"I didn't fall in," said Teddy. "At least, only half of me did," and he began wringing out his scarf. "My feet stopped when they ran into the bricks round the pond," Teddy explained, "but the rest of me didn't."

"Oh, TEDDY!" said Andy, trying not to laugh. "Can you get up again?"

"I don't know," said Teddy, "but I'd rather not try by myself, please, in case the whole of me falls into the pond."

So once more Andy set Teddy on his feet. "Now, wait a minute," he said firmly, as Teddy got ready to rush off again. "You'd better try holding my hand first. Then, when you know how to stop, you can go off by yourself again."

So Andy took Teddy's paw and they skated slowly along the path. Teddy was still rather wobbly, but he felt very proud of himself.

"I'm going to let go of your hand now, Andy," he shouted, and off he went by himself again, though not quite so fast as before.

"Look!" he shouted. "I can turn

corners now," and he vanished round the house.

Rags was just coming out of the door to see what all the noise was about. When he saw Teddy on wheels, he ran up to him, barking and jumping up. Teddy waved his arms.

"Go away, Rags!" he shouted. "Go . . ."

He didn't finish what he was saying because he and Rags were in a heap on the path. Teddy managed to sit up, feeling rather sorry for himself and very tired of falling over so often.

Rags tried to lick his face, and Andy skated down the path towards them.

"It was Rags' fault," said Teddy, rather crossly. "He got in my way," and he glared at the puppy, who tried to lick his face again.

"He's only a puppy," said Andy, "and he didn't know you couldn't stop. And you *were* going rather fast."

Teddy stopped feeling cross. "Yes, I was," he said. "But my skates ran away with me and I can't make them go slowly." He stroked Rags' ears. "I'm going to try just once more, Andy," said Teddy, clambering slowly and carefully to his feet. "Look!" he cried, clapping his paws and nearly losing his balance again. "I got up all by myself!"

"So you did, Teddy," said Andy, laughing. "But you'd better stop clapping your paws, or you'll fall down again. Now, you go once down the path to the gate and back again, and then we'll see if the mincepies are cooked."

Teddy was in a hurry to see the mince-pies, so he skated off down to the gate, still rather wobbly, but less so than before. He quite forgot about not being able to stop until he saw that the gate was open.

"Andy!" he shouted. "Come quickly!"

Andy saw the open gate too, and flew down the path faster than he had ever done before. He passed Teddy just before he reached the gate, and managed to slam it shut.

Andy caught Teddy as he arrived, and stood leaning against the gate to get his breath back.

"That's QUITE enough for one day, Teddy," he said. "I thought you were going right out into the lane."

"So did I at first, Andy," said Teddy, rather breathless too. "Then I heard you coming, so I knew everything would be all right," and he smiled up at

Andy Pandy, who gave him a big hug.

"Well, everything *was* all right this time, but you're never to do it again, will you, Teddy?" said Andy.

Teddy suddenly wrinkled his nose. "What a lovely cooking smell!" he said.

"My mincepies!" shouted Andy. "I'd forgotten all about them. Wait here, Teddy. I'll be back in a minute," and he raced up the path and into the kitchen to take his pies out of the oven. He was in such a hurry that he didn't even shut the door behind him, but rolled straight up to the oven on his skates, and took out the tray of mincepies. They were golden brown and looked as if they would melt in your mouth.

Andy took them out of the tin

"Oh, Teddy," he cried, clutching at him as he flew past.

Andy didn't stop Teddy; he only slowed him down and changed the direction he was going in; so now he was rolling towards the table.

"Andy!" shouted Teddy. "Help!"

and put them on the wire cake-tray to cool.

"I'll just take off my skates, then I'll go and fetch Teddy," he said to himself, sitting down on the floor to undo the straps.

But Teddy had got tired of waiting by the gate. "I'll skate up the path all by myself and surprise Andy," he said. He started off quite slowly, but the skates ran away with him again. By the time he reached the water-butt he was going quite fast, and when he reached the door he was going faster still.

The door was open, so Teddy whizzed through it right into the kitchen. Andy was still sitting on the floor when he saw Teddy coming.

He put his paws out to catch hold of the table, but caught the mincepies instead.

Andy looked at him and burst out laughing. Teddy had a mincepie stuck on each paw.

Teddy laughed too. "Look, Andy—mincepie gloves!" he said. He put out his tongue and licked one of them. "I wish all my gloves were pies," he said.

"No, Teddy," said Andy. "Your paws are all dirty from falling over in the garden. You mustn't eat those mincepies. We'll give them to Rags."

Teddy thought this was a waste. "But

my paws were washed in the pond not long ago," he said, "so they're only a tiny bit dirty."

"You must not eat with paws even a tiny bit dirty," said Andy.

Teddy said, "Rags does."

"Yes," said Andy, "but Rags is a puppy, and puppies are allowed to, but not little bears or little boys."

Teddy was beginning to say that he wished he were a puppy when he saw Andy laughing.

"I don't, REALLY," he said. "If I wash my paws, may I have a mincepie even though it isn't tea-time?"

"Yes," said Andy, "but first sit down and let me take your skates off."

So Teddy washed his paws, and Andy gave him the biggest mincepie of all.

"Andy," said Teddy, with his mouth full, "I got on better than last time, didn't I? Next time," he went on, "I shall be able to skate as well as you. Well, nearly, anyway!"

POTATO ANIMALS

NEEDED: SOME SCRUBBED POTATOES OF DIFFERENT SIZES; THIN STICKS

TO MAKE A HORSE: 1. CHOOSE A BIG POTATO. GIVE IT FOUR STICK-LEGS AND A TAIL

2. THEN TAKE A LITTLE POTATO THIS SHAPE FOR THE HORSE'S HEAD

3. GIVE THE HEAD A STICK-NECK AND TWO LITTLE STICK-EARS. MAKE HOLES FOR THE EYES AND NOSE

HORSE

4. PUSH THE NECK-STICK INTO THE BIG POTATO, AND THERE IS A HORSE

HORSE

CAT

TO MAKE A CAT: 1. CHOOSE A POTATO FLAT AT ONE END SO THAT IT WILL STAND UP. PUSH A SHORT STICK IN AT THE TOP, AND TWO LITTLE LEGS

2. FIND A LITTLE ROUND POTATO. PUSH IN TWO LITTLE PIECES OF STICK FOR EARS. MAKE HOLES FOR THE EYES AND NOSE

3. PUSH THE HEAD ON TO THE STICK ON THE BIG POTATO

TO MAKE A RABBIT: 1. MAKE THIS AS YOU MADE THE CAT, WITH A POTATO THIS SHAPE. ADD A LITTLE TAIL

2. MAKE AS YOU MADE THE CAT, BUT GIVE HIM LONG EARS

The finished cat

3. HERE IS A RABBIT

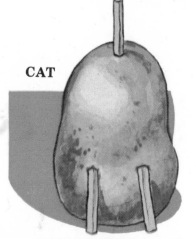
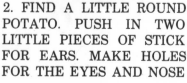

TO MAKE A STORK

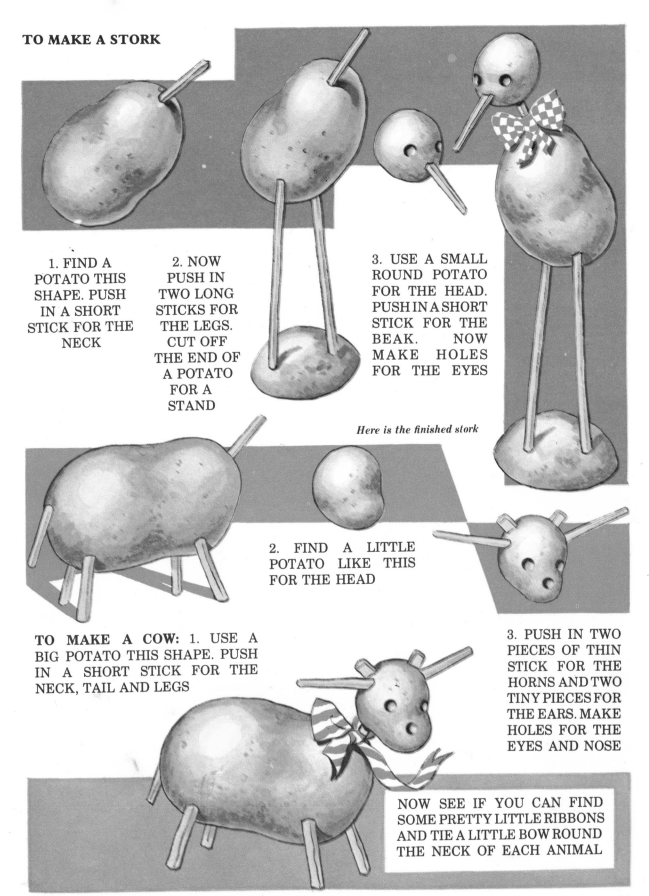

1. FIND A POTATO THIS SHAPE. PUSH IN A SHORT STICK FOR THE NECK

2. NOW PUSH IN TWO LONG STICKS FOR THE LEGS. CUT OFF THE END OF A POTATO FOR A STAND

3. USE A SMALL ROUND POTATO FOR THE HEAD. PUSH IN A SHORT STICK FOR THE BEAK. NOW MAKE HOLES FOR THE EYES

Here is the finished stork

2. FIND A LITTLE POTATO LIKE THIS FOR THE HEAD

TO MAKE A COW: 1. USE A BIG POTATO THIS SHAPE. PUSH IN A SHORT STICK FOR THE NECK, TAIL AND LEGS

3. PUSH IN TWO PIECES OF THIN STICK FOR THE HORNS AND TWO TINY PIECES FOR THE EARS. MAKE HOLES FOR THE EYES AND NOSE

NOW SEE IF YOU CAN FIND SOME PRETTY LITTLE RIBBONS AND TIE A LITTLE BOW ROUND THE NECK OF EACH ANIMAL

DRESSING UP

"It's too wet to play in the garden," said Andy Pandy. "We shall have to stay indoors."

"Let's dress up," said Teddy. They went upstairs to find some dressing-up clothes.

"Who am I being?" asked Andy.

"The postman!" said Teddy.

Teddy began running about on all-fours.

"You're being a bear," said Andy. But Teddy shook his head and began to bark.

"I know!" said Andy. "You're Rags." The real Rags came along. "Now I have two puppies," said Andy.

"My turn," said Andy. He found two brooms and a basket, and knocked at the door.

"You're the man who sells brushes," shouted Teddy, clapping his paws and jumping up and down.

Teddy went to the drawer and took something out.

Can you guess who he was being?

"You won't guess this one," said Andy, going downstairs.

He went into the kitchen. "Who are you being?" asked Teddy. "I'm being me," said Andy.

"Because I'm hungry, and it's nearly tea-time," he went on. So they both turned into themselves again, and had tea.

NO WIND
5
MISS A TURN

6 **7** **8** **9**

FOG
10
BACK TO

4

3

GOOD WIND
2
ON TO **4**

1
↑
START

HOME

SAFELY BACK
32
IN HARBOUR

31 **30** **29**

TEDDY FISHING
28
MISS A TURN

27

EACH PLAYER THROWS A DICE IN TURN AND MOVES THE
NUMBER OF SQUARES THAT TURNS UP. IF HE LANDS ON